LADYBIRD BOOKS, INC.
Auburn, Maine 04210 U.S.A.

LADYBIRD BOOKS, LTD.
Loughborough, Leicestershire, England

Printed in U.S.A.

85

Busy Beavers

PAULINA the PLUMBER

By Cathy East Dubowski
Illustrated by John Speirs

Ladybird Books

It's a beautiful morning! Paulina Beaver is up early. Just as she gets in the shower, the phone rings.

Paulina's workday is about to begin.

Paulina is a plumber—and a busy one, too! She can fix a leaky bathtub, a clogged sink—anything with pipes!

Mrs. Raccoon is on the phone. "We need your help!" she says. "Can you come by soon?"

"Right away!" says Paulina.

But on her way out the door, Paulina
hears, "Help! Help!"
It's Carlton Cat. His lawn sprinkler is out
of control!

Paulina wrestles the sprinkler to the
ground. She has it fixed in no time!
"Oh, thank you," sighs Carlton.

"I've got to run," says Paulina, "I'm already late for another job!"

Paulina heads toward Mrs. Raccoon's house. But halfway down East Street, she spots Olivia Ostrich frantically waving at her to stop.

"Help!" shouts Olivia. "It's an emergency!" Paulina hurries inside.

"M-my diamond ring!" cries Olivia.
"It fell down the drain!"
   Calmly, Paulina turns off the water and
removes the pipe under the sink. "Here's
your ring," she says. "Good as new!"

Finally, Paulina arrives at Mrs. Raccoon's house.

"The toilet is backed up!" says Mrs. Raccoon.

"Don't worry," says Paulina. "I'll have it fixed in no time!"

"It was an accident," says Rocky. "Honest! From now on I'll keep my toys in my room."

At last Paulina arrives at her workshop. Maybe now things will settle down a bit!

But before she has a chance to take off her hat, the phone rings: "Emergency at Woodland Elementary School!"

A water pipe has broken at the elementary school. The whole lunchroom is flooded!

Paulina races down the stairs. "Don't worry!" she says. "I know what to do!"

Everybody cheers—
except Oscar Otter. He
likes having a swimming
pool in the lunchroom!

Just in time, Paulina remembers she has an appointment at Stanley Snake's house! Off she goes to install Stanley's new custom-made bathtub.

"It's s-s-s-splendid!"
says Stanley.

Paulina smiles. She feels very proud when she pleases her customers!

But there's no time to relax today! There's a call on the truck radio: "Trouble at Pine Log Apartments!"

What a sight! The washing machines in the Pine Log Apartments laundry room are overflowing. Water and soap suds are everywhere!

"H-e-e-e-lp!" squawks Lucy Goose. "He-e-e-e-lp!"

Paulina quickly turns off the water and
fixes a twisted drainage hose. "Luckily I
always carry a mop!" she says.

Paulina has promised to do
one more important job today.

She goes to Town Square and gets right
to work on the new fountain.
"Ready?" she asks.
"Ready!" says Mayor Muskrat.
"Now, that's something I'll be proud of
for a long, long time," thinks Paulina happily.

"What a day!" says Paulina as she finally sits down to eat dinner. "It's good to be home where it's nice and quiet."

Paulina is just about to take a sip of soup when she hears...

...*drip, drip, drip...*

"Oh, well," says Paulina, reaching for her tools. "Luckily I know how to fix the faucet myself!"

Here are some of Paulina's favorite tools.

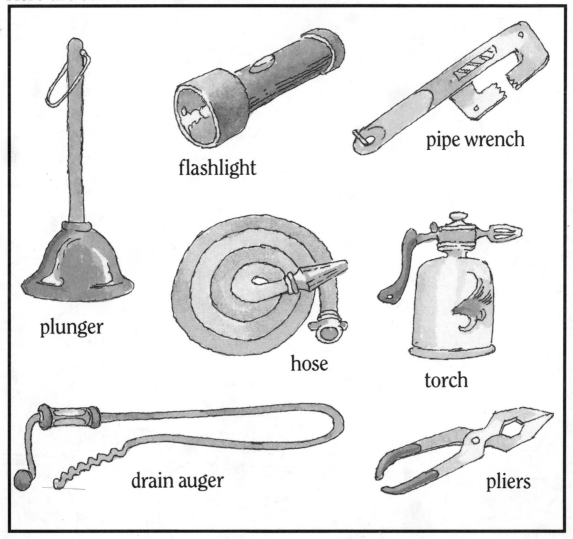

plunger

flashlight

pipe wrench

hose

torch

drain auger

pliers